DATE DUE			
MAY 02 1996			
4/5/00			
NOV 06 2002			

THE ADVENTURES
OF TOM BOMBADIL

BOOKS BY J. R. R. TOLKIEN

The Lord of the Rings:
The Fellowship of the Ring
The Two Towers
The Return of the King

The Hobbit

Farmer Giles of Ham

The Adventures of Tom Bombadil

Smith of Wootton Major

Tree and Leaf

Sir Gawain and the Green Knight,
Pearl and *Sir Orfeo*

The Father Christmas Letters
(edited by Baillie Tolkien)

The Silmarillion
(edited by Christopher Tolkien)

WITH DONALD SWANN
The Road Goes Ever On

J. R. R. TOLKIEN

THE ADVENTURES
OF TOM BOMBADIL

and other verses
from The Red Book

WITH ILLUSTRATIONS BY
PAULINE BAYNES

HOUGHTON MIFFLIN COMPANY BOSTON

1978

ISBN 0–395–26801–X

Printed in the United States of America

A 10 9 8 7 6 5 4 3 2 1

CONTENTS

PREFACE

The Red Book contains a large number of verses. A few are
included in the narrative of the *Downfall of the Lord of the Rings*,
or in the attached stories and chronicles; many more are found on
loose leaves, while some are written carelessly in margins and
blank spaces. Of the last sort most are nonsense, now often
unintelligible even when legible, or half-remembered fragments.
From these marginalia are drawn Nos. 4, 11, 13; though a better
example of their general character would be the scribble, on the
page recording Bilbo's *When winter first begins to bite:*

> *The wind so whirled a weathercock*
> *He could not hold his tail up;*
> *The frost so nipped a throstlecock*
> *He could not snap a snail up.*
> *'My case is hard' the throstle cried,*
> *And 'All is vane' the cock replied;*
> *And so they set their wail up.*

The present selection is taken from the older pieces, mainly
concerned with legends and jests of the Shire at the end of the
Third Age, that appear to have been made by Hobbits, especially
by Bilbo and his friends, or their immediate descendants. Their
authorship is, however, seldom indicated. Those outside the
narratives are in various hands, and were probably written down
from oral tradition.

In the Red Book it is said that No. 5 was made by Bilbo, and
No. 7 by Sam Gamgee. No. 8 is marked SG, and the ascrip-
tion may be accepted. No. 12 is also marked SG, though at most
Sam can only have touched up an older piece of the comic
bestiary lore of which Hobbits appear to have been fond. In
The Lord of the Rings Sam stated that No. 10 was traditional in
the Shire.

No. 3 is an example of another kind which seems to have
amused Hobbits: a rhyme or story which returns to its own
beginning, and so may be recited until the hearers revolt. Several
specimens are found in the Red Book, but the others are simple

and crude. No. 3 is much the longest and most elaborate. It was evidently made by Bilbo. This is indicated by its obvious relationship to the long poem recited by Bilbo, as his own composition, in the house of Elrond. In origin a 'nonsense rhyme', it is in the Rivendell version found transformed and applied, somewhat incongruously, to the High-elvish and Númenorean legends of Eärendil. Probably because Bilbo invented its metrical devices and was proud of them. They do not appear in other pieces in the Red Book. The older form, here given, must belong to the early days after Bilbo's return from his journey. Though the influence of Elvish traditions is seen, they are not seriously treated, and the names used (*Derrilyn, Thellamie, Belmarie, Aerie*) are mere inventions in the Elvish style, and are not in fact Elvish at all.

The influence of the events at the end of the Third Age, and the widening of the horizons of the Shire by contact with Rivendell and Gondor, is to be seen in other pieces. No. 6, though here placed next to Bilbo's Man-in-the-Moon rhyme, and the last item, No. 16, must be derived ultimately from Gondor. They are evidently based on the traditions of Men, living in shorelands and familiar with rivers running into the Sea. No. 6 actually mentions *Belfalas* (the windy bay of Bel), and the Sea-ward Tower, *Tirith Aear*, of Dol Amroth. No. 16 mentions the Seven Rivers[1] that flowed into the Sea in the South Kingdom, and uses the Gondorian name, of High-elvish form, *Fíriel*, mortal woman.[2] In the Langstrand and Dol Amroth there were many traditions of the ancient Elvish dwellings, and of the haven at the mouth of the Morthond from which 'westward ships' had sailed as far back as the fall of Eregion in the Second Age. These two pieces, therefore, are only re-handlings of Southern matter, though this may have reached Bilbo by way of Rivendell. No. 14 also depends on the lore of Rivendell, Elvish and Númenorean, concerning the heroic days at the end of the First Age; it seems to contain echoes of the Númenorean tale of Túrin and Mim the Dwarf.

Nos. 1 and 2 evidently come from the Buckland. They show more knowledge of that country, and of the Dingle, the wooded

---

[1] *Lefnui, Morthond-Kiril-Ringló, Gilrain-Sernui*, and *Anduin*.

[2] The name was borne by a princess of Gondor, through whom Aragorn claimed descent from the Southern line. It was also the name of a daughter of Elanor, daughter of Sam, but her name, if connected with the rhyme, must be derived from it; it could not have arisen in Westmarch.

valley of the Withywindle,[1] than any Hobbits west of the Marish were likely to possess. They also show that the Bucklanders knew Bombadil,[2] though, no doubt, they had as little understanding of his powers as the Shire-folk had of Gandalf's: both were regarded as benevolent persons, mysterious maybe and unpredictable but nonetheless comic. No. 1 is the earlier piece, and is made up of various hobbit-versions of legends concerning Bombadil. No. 2 uses similar traditions, though Tom's raillery is here turned in jest upon his friends, who treat it with amusement (tinged with fear); but it was probably composed much later and after the visit of Frodo and his companions to the house of Bombadil.

The verses, of hobbit origin, here presented have generally two features in common. They are fond of strange words, and of rhyming and metrical tricks—in their simplicity Hobbits evidently regarded such things as virtues or graces, though they were, no doubt, mere imitations of Elvish practices. They are also, at least on the surface, lighthearted or frivolous, though sometimes one may uneasily suspect that more is meant than meets the ear. No. 15, certainly of hobbit origin, is an exception. It is the latest piece and belongs to the Fourth Age; but it is included here, because a hand has scrawled at its head *Frodos Dreme*. That is remarkable, and though the piece is most unlikely to have been written by Frodo himself, the title shows that it was associated with the dark and despairing dreams which visited him in March and October during his last three years. But there were certainly other traditions concerning Hobbits that were taken by the 'wandering-madness', and if they ever returned, were afterwards queer and uncommunicable. The thought of the Sea was ever-present in the background of hobbit imagination; but fear of it and distrust of all Elvish lore, was the prevailing mood in the Shire at the end of the Third Age, and that mood was certainly not entirely dispelled by the events and changes with which that Age ended.

---

[1] *Grindwall* was a small hythe on the north bank of the Withywindle; it was outside the Hay, and so was well watched and protected by a *grind* or fence extended into the water. *Breredon* (Briar Hill) was a little village on rising ground behind the hythe, in the narrow tongue between the end of the High Hay and the Brandywine. At the *Mithe*, the outflow of the Shirebourn, was a landing-stage, from which a lane ran to Deephallow and so on to the Causeway road that went through Rushey and Stock.

[2] Indeed they probably gave him this name (it is Bucklandish in form) to add to his many older ones.

I

THE ADVENTURES OF
TOM BOMBADIL

Old Tom Bombadil was a merry fellow;
bright blue his jacket was and his boots were yellow,
green were his girdle and his breeches all of leather;
he wore in his tall hat a swan-wing feather.
He lived up under Hill, where the Withywindle
ran from a grassy well down into the dingle.

Old Tom in summertime walked about the meadows
gathering the buttercups, running after shadows,
tickling the bumblebees that buzzed among the flowers,
sitting by the waterside for hours upon hours.

There his beard dangled long down into the water:
up came Goldberry, the River-woman's daughter;
pulled Tom's hanging hair. In he went a-wallowing
under the water-lilies, bubbling and a-swallowing.

'Hey, Tom Bombadil! Whither are you going?'
said fair Goldberry. 'Bubbles you are blowing,
frightening the finny fish and the brown water-rat,
startling the dabchicks, and drowning your feather-hat!'

'You bring it back again, there's a pretty maiden!'
said Tom Bombadil. 'I do not care for wading.
Go down! Sleep again where the pools are shady
far below willow-roots, little water-lady!'

Back to her mother's house in the deepest hollow
swam young Goldberry. But Tom, he would not follow;
on knotted willow-roots he sat in sunny weather,
drying his yellow boots and his draggled feather.

Up woke Willow-man, began upon his singing,
sang Tom fast asleep under branches swinging;
in a crack caught him tight: snick! it closed together,
trapped Tom Bombadil, coat and hat and feather.

'Ha, Tom Bombadil! What be you a-thinking,
peeping inside my tree, watching me a-drinking
deep in my wooden house, tickling me with feather,
dripping wet down my face like a rainy weather?'

'You let me out again, Old Man Willow!
I am stiff lying here; they're no sort of pillow,
your hard crooked roots. Drink your river-water!
Go back to sleep again like the River-daughter!'

Willow-man let him loose when he heard him speaking;
locked fast his wooden house, muttering and creaking,
whispering inside the tree. Out from willow-dingle
Tom went walking on up the Withywindle.
Under the forest-eaves he sat a while a-listening:
on the boughs piping birds were chirruping and whistling.
Butterflies about his head went quivering and winking,
until grey clouds came up, as the sun was sinking.

Then Tom hurried on. Rain began to shiver,
round rings spattering in the running river;
a wind blew, shaken leaves chilly drops were dripping;
into a sheltering hole Old Tom went skipping.

Out came Badger-brock with his snowy forehead
and his dark blinking eyes. In the hill he quarried
with his wife and many sons. By the coat they caught him,
pulled him inside their earth, down their tunnels brought him.

Inside their secret house, there they sat a-mumbling:
'Ho, Tom Bombadil! Where have you come tumbling,
bursting in the front-door? Badger-folk have caught you.
You'll never find it out, the way that we have brought you!'

'Now, old Badger-brock, do you hear me talking?
You show me out at once! I must be a-walking.
Show me to your backdoor under briar-roses;
then clean grimy paws, wipe your earthy noses!
Go back to sleep again on your straw pillow,
like fair Goldberry and Old Man Willow!'

Then all the Badger-folk said: 'We beg your pardon!'
They showed Tom out again to their thorny garden,
went back and hid themselves, a-shivering and a-shaking,
blocked up all their doors, earth together raking.

Rain had passed. The sky was clear, and in the summer-
                                                    gloaming
Old Tom Bombadil laughed as he came homing,
unlocked his door again, and opened up a shutter.
In the kitchen round the lamp moths began to flutter;
Tom through the window saw waking stars come winking,
and the new slender moon early westward sinking.

Dark came under Hill. Tom, he lit a candle;
upstairs creaking went, turned the door-handle.
'Hoo, Tom Bombadil! Look what night has brought you!
I'm here behind the door. Now at last I've caught you!
You'd forgotten Barrow-wight dwelling in the old mound
up there on hill-top with the ring of stones round.
He's got loose again. Under earth he'll take you.
Poor Tom Bombadil, pale and cold he'll make you!'

'Go out! Shut the door, and never come back after!
Take away gleaming eyes, take your hollow laughter!
Go back to grassy mound, on your stony pillow
lay down your bony head, like Old Man Willow,

like young Goldberry, and Badger-folk in burrow!
Go back to buried gold and forgotten sorrow!'

Out fled Barrow-wight through the window leaping,
through the yard, over wall like a shadow sweeping,
up hill wailing went back to leaning stone-rings,
back under lonely mound, rattling his bone-rings.

Old Tom Bombadil lay upon his pillow
sweeter than Goldberry, quieter than the Willow,
snugger than the Badger-folk or the Barrow-dwellers;
slept like a humming-top, snored like a bellows.

He woke in morning-light, whistled like a starling,
sang, 'Come, derry-dol, merry-dol, my darling!'
He clapped on his battered hat, boots, and coat and feather;
opened the window wide to the sunny weather.

Wise old Bombadil, he was a wary fellow;
bright blue his jacket was, and his boots were yellow.
None ever caught old Tom in upland or in dingle,
walking the forest-paths, or by the Withywindle,
or out on the lily-pools in boat upon the water.
But one day Tom, he went and caught the River-daughter,
in green gown, flowing hair, sitting in the rushes,
singing old water-songs to birds upon the bushes.

He caught her, held her fast! Water-rats went scuttering
reeds hissed, herons cried, and her heart was fluttering.
Said Tom Bombadil: 'Here's my pretty maiden!
You shall come home with me! The table is all laden:
yellow cream, honeycomb, white bread and butter;
roses at the window-sill and peeping round the shutter.
You shall come under Hill! Never mind your mother
in her deep weedy pool: there you'll find no lover!'

Old Tom Bombadil had a merry wedding,
crowned all with buttercups, hat and feather shedding;
his bride with forgetmenots and flag-lilies for garland
was robed all in silver-green. He sang like a starling,
hummed like a honey-bee, lilted to the fiddle,
clasping his river-maid round her slender middle.

Lamps gleamed within his house, and white was the bedding;
in the bright honey-moon Badger-folk came treading,
danced down under Hill, and Old Man Willow
tapped, tapped at window-pane, as they slept on the pillow,
on the bank in the reeds River-woman sighing
heard old Barrow-wight in his mound crying.

Old Tom Bombadil heeded not the voices,
taps, knocks, dancing feet, all the nightly noises;
slept till the sun arose, then sang like a starling:
'Hey! Come derry-dol, merry-dol, my darling!'
sitting on the door-step chopping sticks of willow,
while fair Goldberry combed her tresses yellow.

2

BOMBADIL GOES BOATING

The old year was turning brown; the West Wind was calling;
Tom caught a beechen leaf in the Forest falling.
'I've caught a happy day blown me by the breezes!
Why wait till morrow-year? I'll take it when me pleases.
This day I'll mend my boat and journey as it chances
west down the withy-stream, following my fancies!'

Little Bird sat on twig. 'Whillo, Tom! I heed you.
I've a guess, I've a guess where your fancies lead you.
Shall I go, shall I go, bring him word to meet you?'

'No names, you tell-tale, or I'll skin and eat you,
babbling in every ear things that don't concern you!
If you tell Willow-man where I've gone, I'll burn you,
roast you on a willow-spit. That'll end your prying!'

Willow-wren cocked her tail, piped as she went flying:
'Catch me first, catch me first! No names are needed.
I'll perch on his hither ear: the message will be heeded.
"Down by Mithe", I'll say, "just as sun is sinking".
Hurry up, hurry up! That's the time for drinking!'

Tom laughed to himself: 'Maybe then I'll go there.
I might go by other ways, but today I'll row there.'
He shaved oars, patched his boat; from hidden creek he
                                                hauled her
through reed and sallow-brake, under leaning alder,
then down the river went, singing: 'Silly-sallow,
Flow withy-willow-stream over deep and shallow!'

'Whee! Tom Bombadil! Whither be you going,
bobbing in a cockle-boat, down the river rowing?'

'Maybe to Brandywine along the Withywindle;
maybe friends of mine fire for me will kindle
down by the Hays-end. Little folk I know there,
kind at the day's end. Now and then I go there'.

'Take word to my kin, bring me back their tidings!
Tell me of diving pools and the fishes' hidings!'

'Nay then', said Bombadil, 'I am only rowing
just to smell the water like, not on errands going'.

'Tee hee! Cocky Tom! Mind your tub don't founder!
Look out for willow-snags! I'd laugh to see you flounder'.

'Talk less, Fisher Blue! Keep your kindly wishes!
Fly off and preen yourself with the bones of fishes!
Gay lord on your bough, at home a dirty varlet
living in a sloven house, though your breast be scarlet.
I've heard of fisher-birds beak in air a-dangling
to show how the wind is set: that's an end of angling!'

The King's fisher shut his beak, winked his eye, as singing
Tom passed under bough. Flash! then he went winging;
dropped down jewel-blue a feather, and Tom caught it
gleaming in a sun-ray: a pretty gift he thought it.
He stuck it in his tall hat, the old feather casting:
'Blue now for Tom', he said, 'a merry hue and lasting!'

Rings swirled round his boat, he saw the bubbles quiver.
Tom slapped his oar, smack! at a shadow in the river.
'Hoosh! Tom Bombadil! 'Tis long since last I met you.
Turned water-boatman, eh? What if I upset you?'

'What? Why, Whisker-lad, I'd ride you down the river.
My fingers on your back would set your hide a-shiver.'

'Pish, Tom Bombadil! I'll go and tell my mother;
"Call all our kin to come, father, sister, brother!
Tom's gone mad as a coot with wooden legs: he's paddling
down Withywindle stream, an old tub a-straddling!"'

'I'll give your otter-fell to Barrow-wights. They'll taw you!
Then smother you in gold-rings! Your mother if she saw you,
she'd never know her son, unless 'twas by a whisker.
Nay, don't tease old Tom, until you be far brisker!'

'Whoosh! said otter-lad, river-water spraying
over Tom's hat and all; set the boat a-swaying,
dived down under it, and by the bank lay peering,
till Tom's merry song faded out of hearing.

Old Swan of Elvet-isle sailed past him proudly,
gave Tom a black look, snorted at him loudly.
Tom laughed: 'You old cob, do you miss your feather?
Give me a new one then! The old was worn by weather.
Could you speak a fair word, I would love you dearer:
long neck and dumb throat, but still a haughty sneerer!
If one day the King returns, in upping he may take you,
brand your yellow bill, and less lordly make you!'
Old Swan huffed his wings, hissed, and paddled faster;
in his wake bobbing on Tom went rowing after.

Tom came to Withy-weir. Down the river rushing
foamed into Windle-reach, a-bubbling and a-splashing;
bore Tom over stone spinning like a windfall,
bobbing like a bottle-cork, to the hythe at Grindwall.

'Hoy! Here's Woodman Tom with his billy-beard on!'
laughed all the little folk of Hays-end and Breredon.
'Ware, Tom! We'll shoot you dead with our bows and arrows!
We don't let Forest-folk nor bogies from the Barrows
cross over Brandywine by cockle-boat nor ferry'.
'Fie, little fatbellies! Don't ye make so merry!

I've seen hobbit-folk digging holes to hide 'em,
frightened if a horny goat or a badger eyed 'em,
afeared of the moony-beams, their own shadows shunning.
I'll call the orks on you: that'll send you running!'

'You may call, Woodman Tom. And you can talk your
                                         beard off.
Three arrows in your hat! You we're not afeared of!
Where would you go to now? If for beer you're making,
the barrels aint deep enough in Breredon for your slaking!'

'Away over Brandywine by Shirebourn I'd be going,
but too swift for cockle-boat the river now is flowing.
I'd bless little folk that took me in their wherry,
wish them evenings fair and many mornings merry'.

Red flowed the Brandywine; with flame the river kindled,
as sun sank beyond the Shire, and then to grey it dwindled.
Mithe Steps empty stood. None was there to greet him.
Silent the Causeway lay. Said Tom: 'A merry meeting!'

Tom stumped along the road, as the light was failing.
Rushey lamps gleamed ahead. He heard a voice him hailing.
'Whoa there!' Ponies stopped, wheels halted sliding.
Tom went plodding past, never looked beside him.

'Ho there! beggarman tramping in the Marish!
What's your business here? Hat all stuck with arrows!
Someone's warned you off, caught you at your sneaking?
Come here! Tell me now what it is you're seeking!
Shire-ale, I'll be bound, though you've not a penny.
I'll bid them lock their doors, and then you won't get any!'

'Well, well, Muddy-feet! From one that's late for meeting
away back by the Mithe that's a surly greeting!
You old farmer fat that cannot walk for wheezing,
cart-drawn like a sack, ought to be more pleasing.

Penny-wise tub-on-legs! A beggar can't be chooser,
or else I'd bid you go, and you would be the loser.
Come, Maggot! Help me up! A tankard now you owe me.
Even in cockshut light an old friend should know me!'

Laughing they drove away, in Rushey never halting,
though the inn open stood and they could smell the malting.
They turned down Maggot's Lane, rattling and bumping,
Tom in the farmer's cart dancing round and jumping.
Stars shone on Bamfurlong, and Maggot's house was lighted;
fire in the kitchen burned to welcome the benighted.

Maggot's sons bowed at door, his daughters did their curtsy,
his wife brought tankards out for those that might be thirsty.
Songs they had and merry tales, the supping and the dancing;
Goodman Maggot there for all his belt was prancing,
Tom did a hornpipe when he was not quaffing,
daughters did the Springle-ring, goodwife did the laughing.

When others went to bed in hay, fern, or feather,
close in the inglenook they laid their heads together,
old Tom and Muddy-feet, swapping all the tidings
from Barrow-downs to Tower Hills: of walkings and of
                                                    ridings;
of wheat-ear and barley-corn, of sowing and of reaping;
queer tales from Bree, and talk at smithy, mill, and cheaping;
rumours in whispering trees, south-wind in the larches,
tall Watchers by the Ford, Shadows on the marches.

Old Maggot slept at last in chair beside the embers.
Ere dawn Tom was gone: as dreams one half remembers,
some merry, some sad, and some of hidden warning.
None heard the door unlocked; a shower of rain at morning
his footprints washed away, at Mithe he left no traces,
at Hays-end they heard no song nor sound of heavy paces.

Three days his boat lay by the hythe at Grindwall,
and then one morn was gone back up Withywindle.
Otter-folk, hobbits said, came by night and loosed her,
dragged her over weir, and up stream they pushed her.

Out from Elvet-isle Old Swan came sailing,
in beak took her painter up in the water trailing,
drew her proudly on; otters swam beside her
round old Willow-man's crooked roots to guide her;
the King's fisher perched on bow, on thwart the wren was
singing,
merrily the cockle-boat homeward they were bringing.
To Tom's creek they came at last. Otter-lad said: 'Whish now!
What's a coot without his legs, or a finless fish now?'
O! silly-sallow-willow-stream! The oars they'd left behind
them!
Long they lay at Grindwall hythe for Tom to come and find
them.

3

ERRANTRY

There was a merry passenger,
a messenger, a mariner:
he built a gilded gondola
to wander in, and had in her
a load of yellow oranges
and porridge for his provender;
he perfumed her with marjoram
and cardamom and lavender.

He called the winds of argosies
with cargoes in to carry him
across the rivers seventeen
that lay between to tarry him.
He landed all in loneliness
where stonily the pebbles on
the running river Derrilyn
goes merrily for ever on.
He journeyed then through meadow-lands
to Shadow-land that dreary lay,
and under hill and over hill
went roving still a weary way.

He sat and sang a melody,
his errantry a-tarrying;
he begged a pretty butterfly
that fluttered by to marry him.
She scorned him and she scoffed at him,
she laughed at him unpitying;
so long he studied wizardry
and sigaldry and smithying.

He wove a tissue airy-thin
to snare her in; to follow her
he made him beetle-leather wing
and feather wing of swallow-hair.
He caught her in bewilderment
with filament of spider-thread;
he made her soft pavilions
of lilies, and a bridal bed
of flowers and of thistle-down
to nestle down and rest her in;
and silken webs of filmy white
and silver light he dressed her in.

He threaded gems in necklaces,
but recklessly she squandered them
and fell to bitter quarrelling;
then sorrowing he wandered on,
and there he left her withering,
as shivering he fled away;
with windy weather following
on swallow-wing he sped away.

He passed the archipelagoes
where yellow grows the marigold,
where countless silver fountains are,
and mountains are of fairy-gold.
He took to war and foraying,
a-harrying beyond the sea,
and roaming over Belmarie
and Thellamie and Fantasie.

He made a shield and morion
of coral and of ivory,
a sword he made of emerald,
and terrible his rivalry
with elven-knights of Aerie
and Faerie, with paladins

that golden-haired and shining-eyed
came riding by and challenged him.

Of crystal was his habergeon,
his scabbard of chalcedony;
with silver tipped at plenilune
his spear was hewn of ebony.
His javelins were of malachite
and stalactite—he brandished them,
and went and fought the dragon-flies
of Paradise, and vanquished them.

He battled with the Dumbledors,
the Hummerhorns, and Honeybees,
and won the Golden Honeycomb;
and running home on sunny seas ·
in ship of leaves and gossamer
with blossom for a canopy,
he sat and sang, and furbished up
and burnished up his panoply.

He tarried for a little while
in little isles that lonely lay,
and found there naught but blowing grass;
and so at last the only way
he took, and turned, and coming home
with honeycomb, to memory
his message came, and errand too!
In derring-do and glamoury
he had forgot them, journeying
and tourneying, a wanderer.
So now he must depart again
and start again his gondola,
for ever still a messenger,
a passenger, a tarrier,
a-roving as a feather does,
a weather-driven mariner.

4

PRINCESS MEE

Little Princess Mee
Lovely was she
As in elven-song is told:
She had pearls in hair
All threaded fair;
Of gossamer shot with gold
Was her kerchief made,
And a silver braid
Of stars about her throat.
Of moth-web light
All moonlit-white
She wore a woven coat,
And round her kirtle
Was bound a girdle
Sewn with diamond dew.

She walked by day
Under mantle grey
And hood of clouded blue;
But she went by night
All glittering bright
Under the starlit sky,
And her slippers frail
Of fishes' mail
Flashed as she went by
To her dancing-pool,
And on mirror cool
Of windless water played.
As a mist of light
In whirling flight

A glint like glass she made
    Wherever her feet
    Of silver fleet
Flicked the dancing-floor.

    She looked on high
    To the roofless sky,
And she looked to the shadowy shore;
    Then round she went,
    And her eyes she bent
And saw beneath her go
    A Princess Shee
    As fair as Mee:
They were dancing toe to toe!

    Shee was as light
    As Mee, and as bright;
But Shee was, strange to tell,
    Hanging down
    With starry crown
Into a bottomless well!
    Her gleaming eyes
    In great surprise
Looked up to the eyes of Mee:
    A marvellous thing,
    Head-down to swing
Above a starry sea!

    Only their feet
    Could ever meet;
For where the ways might lie
    To find a land
    Where they do not stand
But hang down in the sky
    No one could tell
    Nor learn in spell
In all the elven-lore.

So still on her own
    An elf alone
Dancing as before
    With pearls in hair
    And kirtle fair
    And slippers frail
    Of fishes' mail went Mee:
    Of fishes' mail
    And slippers frail
    And kirtle fair
With pearls in hair went Shee!

5

THE MAN IN THE MOON
STAYED UP TOO LATE

There is an inn, a merry old inn
  beneath an old grey hill,
And there they brew a beer so brown
That the Man in the Moon himself came down
  one night to drink his fill.

The ostler has a tipsy cat
  that plays a five-stringed fiddle;
And up and down he runs his bow,
Now squeaking high, now purring low,
  now sawing in the middle.

The landlord keeps a little dog
  that is mighty fond of jokes;
When there's good cheer among the guests,
He cocks an ear at all the jests
  and laughs until he chokes.

They also keep a hornéd cow
  as proud as any queen;
But music turns her head like ale,
And makes her wave her tufted tail
  and dance upon the green.

And O! the row of silver dishes
  and the store of silver spoons!
For Sunday there's a special pair,
And these they polish up with care
  on Saturday afternoons.

The Man in the Moon was drinking deep,
   and the cat began to wail;
A dish and a spoon on the table danced,
The cow in the garden madly pranced,
   and the little dog chased his tail.

The Man in the Moon took another mug,
   and then rolled beneath his chair;
And there he dozed and dreamed of ale,
Till in the sky the stars were pale,
   and dawn was in the air.

The ostler said to his tipsy cat:
   'The white horses of the Moon,
They neigh and champ their silver bits;
But their master's been and drowned his wits,
   and the Sun'll be rising soon!'

So the cat on his fiddle played hey-diddle-diddle,
   a jig that would wake the dead:
He squeaked and sawed and quickened the tune,
While the landlord shook the Man in the Moon:
   'It's after three!' he said.

They rolled the Man slowly up the hill
   and bundled him into the Moon,
While his horses galloped up in rear,
And the cow came capering like a deer,
   and a dish ran up with a spoon.

Now quicker the fiddle went deedle-dum-diddle;
   the dog began to roar,
The cow and the horses stood on their heads;
The guests all bounded from their beds
   and danced upon the floor.

With a ping and a pong the fiddle-strings broke!
   the cow jumped over the Moon,

And the little dog laughed to see such fun,
And the Saturday dish went off at a run
　with the silver Sunday spoon.

The round Moon rolled behind the hill,
　as the Sun raised up her head.
She hardly believed her fiery eyes;
For though it was day, to her surprise
　they all went back to bed!

6
THE MAN IN THE MOON
CAME DOWN TOO SOON

The Man in the Moon had silver shoon,
    and his beard was of silver thread;
With opals crowned and pearls all bound
    about his girdlestead,
In his mantle grey he walked one day
    across a shining floor,
And with crystal key in secrecy
    he opened an ivory door.

On a filigree stair of glimmering hair
    then lightly down he went,
And merry was he at last to be free
    on a mad adventure bent.
In diamonds white he had lost delight;
    he was tired of his minaret
Of tall moonstone that towered alone
    on a lunar mountain set.

He would dare any peril for ruby and beryl
    to broider his pale attire,
For new diadems of lustrous gems,
    emerald and sapphire.
He was lonely too with nothing to do
    but stare at the world of gold
And heark to the hum that would distantly come
    as gaily round it rolled.

At plenilune in his argent moon
   in his heart he longed for Fire:
Not the limpid lights of wan selenites;
   for red was his desire,
For crimson and rose and ember-glows,
   for flame with burning tongue,
For the scarlet skies in a swift sunrise
   when a stormy day is young.

He'd have seas of blues, and the living hues
   of forest green and fen;
And he yearned for the mirth of the populous earth
   and the sanguine blood of men.
He coveted song, and laughter long,
   and viands hot, and wine,
Eating pearly cakes of light snowflakes
   and drinking thin moonshine.

He twinkled his feet, as he thought of the meat,
   of pepper, and punch galore;
And he tripped unaware on his slanting stair,
   and like a meteor,
A star in flight, ere Yule one night
   flickering down he fell
From his laddery path to a foaming bath
   in the windy Bay of Bel.

He began to think, lest he melt and sink,
   what in the moon to do,
When a fisherman's boat found him far afloat
   to the amazement of the crew,
Caught in their net all shimmering wet
   in a phosphorescent sheen
Of bluey whites and opal lights
   and delicate liquid green.

Against his wish with the morning fish
   they packed him back to land:

'You had best get a bed in an inn', they said;
  'the town is near at hand'.
Only the knell of one slow bell
  high in the Seaward Tower
Announced the news of his moonsick cruise
  at that unseemly hour.

Not a hearth was laid, not a breakfast made,
  and dawn was cold and damp.
There were ashes for fire, and for grass the mire,
  for the sun a smoking lamp
In a dim back-street. Not a man did he meet,
  no voice was raised in song;
There were snores instead, for all folk were abed
  and still would slumber long.

He knocked as he passed on doors locked fast,
  and called and cried in vain,
Till he came to an inn that had light within,
  and tapped at a window-pane.
A drowsy cook gave a surly look,
  and 'What do you want?' said he.
'I want fire and gold and songs of old
  and red wine flowing free!'

'You won't get them here', said the cook with a leer,
  'but you may come inside.
Silver I lack and silk to my back—
  maybe I'll let you bide'.
A silver gift the latch to lift,
  a pearl to pass the door;
For a seat by the cook in the ingle-nook
  it cost him twenty more.

For hunger or drouth naught passed his mouth
  till he gave both crown and cloak;
And all that he got, in an earthen pot
  broken and black with smoke,

Was porridge cold and two days old
   to eat with a wooden spoon.
For puddings of Yule with plums, poor fool,
   he arrived so much too soon:
An unwary guest on a lunatic quest
   from the Mountains of the Moon.

7
THE STONE TROLL

Troll sat alone on his seat of stone,
And munched and mumbled a bare old bone;
  For many a year he had gnawed it near,
    For meat was hard to come by.
      Done by! Gum by!
  In a cave in the hills he dwelt alone,
    And meat was hard to come by.

Up came Tom with his big boots on.
Said he to Troll: 'Pray, what is yon?
  For it looks like the shin o' my nuncle Tim,
    As should be a-lyin' in graveyard.
      Caveyard! Paveyard!
  This many a year has Tim been gone,
    And I thought he were lyin' in graveyard'.

'My lad', said Troll, 'this bone I stole.
But what be bones that lie in a hole?
  Thy nuncle was dead as a lump o' lead,
    Afore I found his shinbone.
      Tinbone! Thinbone!
  He can spare a share for a poor old troll;
    For he don't need his shinbone'.

Said Tom: 'I don't see why the likes o' thee
Without axin' leave should go makin' free
  With the shank or the shin o' my father's kin;
    So hand the old bone over!
      Rover! Trover!
  Though dead he be, it belongs to he;
    So hand the old bone over!'

'For a couple o' pins', says Troll, and grins,
'I'll eat thee too, and gnaw thy shins.
    A bit o' fresh meat will go down sweet!
        I'll try my teeth on thee now.
            Hee now! See now!
    I'm tired o' gnawing old bones and skins;
        I've a mind to dine on thee now'.

But just as he thought his dinner was caught,
He found his hands had hold of naught.
    Before he could mind, Tom slipped behind
        And gave him the boot to larn him.
            Warn him! Darn him!
    A bump o' the boot on the seat, Tom thought,
        Would be the way to larn him.

But harder than stone is the flesh and bone
Of a troll that sits in the hills alone.
    As well set your boot to the mountain's root,
        For the seat of a troll don't feel it.
            Peel it! Heal it!
    Old Troll laughed, when he heard Tom groan,
        And he knew his toes could feel it.

Tom's leg is game, since home he came,
And his bootless foot is lasting lame;
    But Troll don't care, and he's still there
        With the bone he boned from its owner.
            Doner! Boner!
    Troll's old seat is still the same,
        And the bone he boned from its owner!

8

PERRY-THE-WINKLE

The Lonely Troll he sat on a stone
   and sang a mournful lay:
'O why, O why must I live on my own
   in the hills of Faraway?
My folk are gone beyond recall
   and take no thought of me;
alone I'm left, the last of all
   from Weathertop to the Sea'.

'I steal no gold, I drink no beer,
   I eat no kind of meat;
but People slam their doors in fear,
   whenever they hear my feet.
O how I wish that they were neat,
   and my hands were not so rough!
Yet my heart is soft, my smile is sweet,
   and my cooking good enough.'

'Come, come!' he thought, 'this will not do!
   I must go and find a friend;
a-walking soft I'll wander through
   the Shire from end to end'.
Down he went, and he walked all night
   with his feet in boots of fur;
to Delving he came in the morning light,
   when folk were just astir.

He looked around, and who did he meet
   but old Mrs. Bunce and all
with umbrella and basket walking the street;
   and he smiled and stopped to call:

'Good morning, ma'am! Good day to you!
   I hope I find you well?'
But she dropped umbrella and basket too,
   and yelled a frightful yell.

Old Pott the Mayor was strolling near;
   when he heard that awful sound,
he turned all purple and pink with fear,
   and dived down underground.

The Lonely Troll was hurt and sad:
   'Don't go!' he gently said,
but old Mrs. Bunce ran home like mad
   and hid beneath her bed.

The Troll went on to the market-place
   and peeped above the stalls;
the sheep went wild when they saw his face,
   and the geese flew over the walls.
Old Farmer Hogg he spilled his ale,
   Bill Butcher threw a knife,
and Grip his dog, he turned his tail
   and ran to save his life.

The old Troll sadly sat and wept
   outside the Lockholes gate,
and Perry-the-Winkle up he crept
   and patted him on the pate.
'O why do you weep, you great big lump?
   You're better outside than in!'
He gave the Troll a friendly thump,
   and laughed to see him grin.

'O Perry-the-Winkle boy', he cried,
   'come, you're the lad for me!
Now if you're willing to take a ride,
   I'll carry you home to tea'.

He jumped on his back and held on tight,
    and 'Off you go!' said he;
and the Winkle had a feast that night,
    and sat on the old Troll's knee.

There were pikelets, there was buttered toast,
    and jam, and cream, and cake,
and the Winkle strove to eat the most,
    though his buttons all should break.
The kettle sang, the fire was hot,
    the pot was large and brown,
and the Winkle tried to drink the lot,
    in tea though he should drown.

When full and tight were coat and skin,
    they rested without speech,
till the old Troll said: 'I'll now begin
    the baker's art to teach,
the making of beautiful cramsome bread,
    of bannocks light and brown;
and then you can sleep on a heather-bed
    with pillows of owlets' down'.

'Young Winkle, where've you been?' they said.
    'I've been to a fulsome tea,
and I feel so fat, for I have fed
    on cramsome bread', said he.
'But where, my lad, in the Shire was that?
    Or out in Bree?' said they.
But Winkle he up and answered flat:
    'I aint a-going to say'.

'But I know where', said Peeping Jack,
    'I watched him ride away:
he went upon the old Troll's back
    to the hills of Faraway'.
Then all the People went with a will,

by pony, cart, or moke,
until they came to a house in a hill
and saw a chimney smoke.

They hammered upon the old Troll's door.
  'A beautiful cramsome cake
O bake for us, please, or two, or more;
  O bake!' they cried, 'O bake!'
'Go home, go home!' the old Troll said.
  'I never invited you.
Only on Thursdays I bake my bread,
  and only for a few'.

'Go home! Go home! There's some mistake.
  My house is far too small;
and I've no pikelets, cream, or cake:
  the Winkle has eaten all!
You Jack, and Hogg, old Bunce and Pott
  I wish no more to see.
Be off! Be off now all the lot!
  The Winkle's the boy for me!'

Now Perry-the-Winkle grew so fat
  through eating of cramsome bread,
his weskit bust, and never a hat
  would sit upon his head;
for Every Thursday he went to tea,
  and sat on the kitchen floor,
and smaller the old Troll seemed to be,
  as he grew more and more.

The Winkle a Baker great became,
  as still is said in song;
from the Sea to Bree there went the fame
  of his bread both short and long.
But it weren't so good as the cramsome bread:
  no butter so rich and free,
as Every Thursday the old Troll spread
  for Perry-the-Winkle's tea.

9
THE MEWLIPS

The shadows where the Mewlips dwell
  Are dark and wet as ink,
And slow and softly rings their bell,
  As in the slime you sink.

You sink into the slime, who dare
  To knock upon their door,
While down the grinning gargoyles stare
  And noisome waters pour.

Beside the rotting river-strand
  The drooping willows weep,
And gloomily the gorcrows stand
  Croaking in their sleep.

Over the Merlock Mountains a long and weary way,
  In a mouldy valley where the trees are grey,
By a dark pool's borders without wind or tide,
  Moonless and sunless, the Mewlips hide.

The cellars where the Mewlips sit
  Are deep and dank and cold
With single sickly candle lit;
  And there they count their gold.

Their walls are wet, their ceilings drip;
  Their feet upon the floor
Go softly with a squish-flap-flip,
  As they sidle to the door.

They peep out slyly; through a crack
    Their feeling fingers creep,
And when they've finished, in a sack
    Your bones they take to keep.

Beyond the Merlock Mountains, a long and lonely road,
    Through the spider-shadows and the marsh of Tode,
And through the wood of hanging trees and the gallows-
                                                weed,
    You go to find the Mewlips—and the Mewlips feed.

10
OLIPHAUNT

Grey as a mouse,
Big as a house,
Nose like a snake,
I make the earth shake,
As I tramp through the grass;
Trees crack as I pass.
With horns in my mouth
I walk in the South,
Flapping big ears.
Beyond count of years
I stump round and round,
Never lie on the ground,
Not even to die.
Oliphaunt am I,
Biggest of all,
Huge, old, and tall.
If ever you'd met me,
You wouldn't forget me.
If you never do,
You won't think I'm true;
But old Oliphaunt am I,
And I never lie.

II

FASTITOCALON

Look, there is Fastitocalon!
An island good to land upon,
　　Although 'tis rather bare.
Come, leave the sea! And let us run,
Or dance, or lie down in the sun!
　　　See, gulls are sitting there!
　　　　　　Beware!
　　　Gulls do not sink.
There they may sit, or strut and prink:
Their part it is to tip the wink,
　　If anyone should dare
　　Upon that isle to settle,
Or only for a while to get
Relief from sickness or the wet,
　　Or maybe boil a kettle.

Ah! foolish folk, who land on HIM,
And little fires proceed to trim
　　And hope perhaps for tea!
It may be that His shell is thick,
He seems to sleep; but He is quick,
　　And floats now in the sea
　　　　　With guile;
And when He hears their tapping feet,
Or faintly feels the sudden heat,
　　　　　With smile
　　　　　HE dives,
And promptly turning upside-down
He tips them off, and deep they drown,
　　And lose their silly lives
　　　　To their surprise.

Be wise!
There are many monsters in the Sea,
But none so perilous as HE,
Old horny Fastitocalon,
Whose mighty kindred all have gone,
The last of the old Turtle-fish.
So if to save your life you wish
    Then I advise:
Pay heed to sailors' ancient lore,
Set foot on no uncharted shore!
    Or better still,
Your days at peace on Middle-earth
        In mirth
        Fulfill!

12
CAT

The fat cat on the mat
  may seem to dream
of nice mice that suffice
  for him, or cream;
but he free, maybe,
  walks in thought
unbowed, proud, where loud
  roared and fought
his kin, lean and slim,
  or deep in den
in the East feasted on beasts
  and tender men.

The giant lion with iron
  claw in paw,
and huge ruthless tooth
  in gory jaw;
the pard dark-starred,
  fleet upon feet,
that oft soft from aloft
  leaps on his meat
where woods loom in gloom—
  far now they be,
  fierce and free,
  and tamed is he;
but fat cat on the mat
  kept as a pet,
  he does not forget.

13

SHADOW-BRIDE

There was a man who dwelt alone,
   as day and night went past
he sat as still as carven stone,
   and yet no shadow cast.
The white owls perched upon his head
   beneath the winter moon;
they wiped their beaks and thought him dead
   under the stars of June.

There came a lady clad in grey
   in the twilight shining:
one moment she would stand and stay,
   her hair with flowers entwining.
He woke, as had he sprung of stone,
   and broke the spell that bound him;
he clasped her fast, both flesh and bone,
   and wrapped her shadow round him.

There never more she walks her ways
   by sun or moon or star;
she dwells below where neither days
   nor any nights there are.
But once a year when caverns yawn
   and hidden things awake,
they dance together then till dawn
   and a single shadow make.

14

THE HOARD

When the moon was new and the sun young
of silver and gold the gods sung:
in the green grass they silver spilled,
and the white waters they with gold filled.
Ere the pit was dug or Hell yawned,
ere dwarf was bred or dragon spawned,
there were Elves of old, and strong spells
under green hills in hollow dells
they sang as they wrought many fair things,
and the bright crowns of the Elf-kings.
But their doom fell, and their song waned,
by iron hewn and by steel chained.
Greed that sang not, nor with mouth smiled,
in dark holes their wealth piled,
graven silver and carven gold:
over Elvenhome the shadow rolled.

There was an old dwarf in a dark cave,
to silver and gold his fingers clave;
with hammer and tongs and anvil-stone
he worked his hands to the hard bone,
and coins he made, and strings of rings,
and thought to buy the power of kings.
But his eyes grew dim and his ears dull
and the skin yellow on his old skull;
through his bony claw with a pale sheen
the stony jewels slipped unseen.
No feet he heard, though the earth quaked,
when the young dragon his thirst slaked,

and the stream smoked at his dark door.
The flames hissed on the dank floor.
and he died alone in the red fire;
his bones were ashes in the hot mire.

There was an old dragon under grey stone;
his red eyes blinked as he lay alone.
His joy was dead and his youth spent,
he was knobbed and wrinkled, and his limbs bent
in the long years to his gold chained;
in his heart's furnace the fire waned.
To his belly's slime gems stuck thick,
silver and gold he would snuff and lick:
he knew the place of the least ring
beneath the shadow of his black wing.
Of thieves he thought on his hard bed,
and dreamed that on their flesh he fed,
their bones crushed, and their blood drank:
his ears drooped and his breath sank.
Mail-rings rang. He heard them not.
A voice echoed in his deep grot:
a young warrior with a bright sword
called him forth to defend his hoard.
His teeth were knives, and of horn his hide,
but iron tore him, and his flame died.

There was an old king on a high throne:
his white beard lay on knees of bone;
his mouth savoured neither meat nor drink,
nor his ears song; he could only think
of his huge chest with carven lid
where pale gems and gold lay hid
in secret treasury in the dark ground;
its strong doors were iron-bound.
The swords of his thanes were dull with rust,
his glory fallen, his rule unjust,
his halls hollow, and his bowers cold,
but king he was of elvish gold.

He heard not the horns in the mountain-pass,
he smelt not the blood on the trodden grass,
but his halls were burned, his kingdom lost;
in a cold pit his bones were tossed.

There is an old hoard in a dark rock,
forgotten behind doors none can unlock;
that grim gate no man can pass.
On the mound grows the green grass;
there sheep feed and the larks soar,
and the wind blows from the sea-shore.
The old hoard the Night shall keep,
while earth waits and the Elves sleep.

15

THE SEA-BELL

I walked by the sea, and there came to me,
  as a star-beam on the wet sand,
a white shell like a sea-bell;
  trembling it lay in my wet hand.
In my fingers shaken I heard waken
  a ding within, by a harbour bar
a buoy swinging, a call ringing
  over endless seas, faint now and far.

Then I saw a boat silently float
  on the night-tide, empty and grey.
'It is later than late! Why do we wait?'
  I leapt in and cried: 'Bear me away!'

It bore me away, wetted with spray,
  wrapped in a mist, wound in a sleep,
to a forgotten strand in a strange land.
  In the twilight beyond the deep
I heard a sea-bell swing in the swell,
  dinging, dinging, and the breakers roar
on the hidden teeth of a perilous reef;
  and at last I came to a long shore.
White it glimmered, and the sea simmered
  with star-mirrors in a silver net;
cliffs of stone pale as ruel-bone
  in the moon-foam were gleaming wet.
Glittering sand slid through my hand,
  dust of pearl and jewel-grist,
trumpets of opal, roses of coral,
  flutes of green and amethyst.

But under cliff-eaves there were glooming caves,
     weed-curtained, dark and grey;
a cold air stirred in my hair,
     and the light waned, as I hurried away.

Down from a hill ran a green rill;
     its water I drank to my heart's ease.
Up its fountain-stair to a country fair
     of ever-eve I came, far from the seas,
climbing into meadows of fluttering shadows:
     flowers lay there like fallen stars,
and on a blue pool, glassy and cool,
     like floating moons the nenuphars.
Alders were sleeping, and willows weeping
     by a slow river of rippling weeds;
gladdon-swords guarded the fords,
     and green spears, and arrow-reeds.

There was echo of song all the evening long
     down in the valley; many a thing
running to and fro: hares white as snow,
     voles out of holes; moths on the wing
with lantern-eyes; in quiet surprise
     brocks were staring out of dark doors.
I heard dancing there, music in the air,
     feet going quick on the green floors.
But wherever I came it was ever the same:
     the feet fled, and all was still;
never a greeting, only the fleeting
     pipes, voices, horns on the hill.

Of river-leaves and the rush-sheaves
     I made me a mantle of jewel-green,
a tall wand to hold, and a flag of gold;
     my eyes shone like the star-sheen.
With flowers crowned I stood on a mound,
     and shrill as a call at cock-crow

proudly I cried: 'Why do you hide?
  Why do none speak, wherever I go?
Here now I stand, king of this land,
  with gladdon-sword and reed-mace.
Answer my call! Come forth all!
  Speak to me words! Show me a face!'

Black came a cloud as a night-shroud.
  Like a dark mole groping I went,
to the ground falling, on my hands crawling
  with eyes blind and my back bent.
I crept to a wood: silent it stood
  in its dead leaves; bare were its boughs.
There must I sit, wandering in wit,
  while owls snored in their hollow house.
For a year and a day there must I stay:
  beetles were tapping in the rotten trees,
spiders were weaving, in the mould heaving
  puffballs loomed about my knees.

At last there came light in my long night,
  and I saw my hair hanging grey.
'Bent though I be, I must find the sea!
  I have lost myself, and I know not the way,
but let me be gone!' Then I stumbled on;
  like a hunting bat shadow was over me;
in my ears dinned a withering wind,
  and with ragged briars I tried to cover me.
My hands were torn and my knees worn,
  and years were heavy upon my back,
when the rain in my face took a salt taste,
  and I smelled the smell of sea-wrack.

Birds came sailing, mewing, wailing;
  I heard voices in cold caves,
seals barking, and rocks snarling,
  and in spout-holes the gulping of waves.

Winter came fast; into a mist I passed,
    to land's end my years I bore;
snow was in the air, ice in my hair,
    darkness was lying on the last shore.

'There still afloat waited the boat,
    in the tide lifting, its prow tossing.
Weary I lay, as it bore me away,
    the waves climbing, the seas crossing,
passing old hulls clustered with gulls
    and great ships laden with light,
coming to haven, dark as a raven,
    silent as snow, deep in the night.

Houses were shuttered, wind round them muttered,
    roads were empty. I sat by a door,
and where drizzling rain poured down a drain
    I cast away all that I bore:
in my clutching hand some grains of sand,
    and a sea-shell silent and dead.
Never will my ear that bell hear,
    never my feet that shore tread,
never again, as in sad lane,
    in blind alley and in long street
ragged I walk. To myself I talk;
    for still they speak not, men that I meet.

16

THE LAST SHIP

Fíriel looked out at three o'clock:
 the grey night was going;
far away a golden cock
 clear and shrill was crowing.
The trees were dark, and the dawn pale,
 waking birds were cheeping,
a wind moved cool and frail
 through dim leaves creeping.

She watched the gleam at window grow,
 till the long light was shimmering
on land and leaf; on grass below
 grey dew was glimmering.
Over the floor her white feet crept,
 down the stair they twinkled,
through the grass they dancing stepped
 all with dew besprinkled.

Her gown had jewels upon its hem,
 as she ran down to the river,
and leaned upon a willow-stem,
 and watched the water quiver.
A kingfisher plunged down like a stone
 in a blue flash falling,
bending reeds were softly blown,
 lily-leaves were sprawling.

A sudden music to her came,
 as she stood there gleaming
with free hair in the morning's flame
 on her shoulders streaming.

Flutes there were, and harps were wrung,
  and there was sound of singing,
like wind-voices keen and young
  and far bells ringing.

A ship with golden beak and oar
  and timbers white came gliding;
swans went sailing on before,
  her tall prow guiding.
Fair folk out of Elvenland
  in silver-grey were rowing,
and three with crowns she saw there stand
  with bright hair flowing.

With harp in hand they sang their song
  to the slow oars swinging:
'Green is the land, the leaves are long,
  and the birds are singing.
Many a day with dawn of gold
  this earth will lighten,
many a flower will yet unfold,
  ere the cornfields whiten.

'Then whither go ye, boatmen fair,
  down the river gliding?
To twilight and to secret lair
  in the great forest hiding?
To Northern isles and shores of stone
  on strong swans flying,
by cold waves to dwell alone
  with the white gulls crying?'

'Nay!' they answered. 'Far away
  on the last road faring,
leaving western havens grey,
  the seas of shadow daring,

we go back to Elvenhome,
    where the White Tree is growing,
and the Star shines upon the foam
    on the last shore flowing.

'To mortal fields say farewell,
    Middle-earth forsaking!
In Elvenhome a clear bell
    in the high tower is shaking.
Here grass fades and leaves fall,
    and sun and moon wither,
and we have heard the far call
    that bids us journey thither'.

The oars were stayed. They turned aside:
    'Do you hear the call, Earth-maiden?
Fíriel! Fíriel!' they cried.
    'Our ship is not full-laden.
One more only we may bear.
    Come! For your days are speeding.
Come! Earth-maiden elven-fair,
    our last call heeding.'

Fíriel looked from the river-bank,
    one step daring;
then deep in clay her feet sank,
    and she halted staring.
Slowly the elven-ship went by
    whispering through the water:
'I cannot come!' they heard her cry.
    'I was born Earth's daughter!'

No jewels bright her gown bore,
    as she walked back from the meadow
under roof and dark door,
    under the house-shadow.

She donned her smock of russet brown,
    her long hair braided,
and to her work came stepping down.
    Soon the sunlight faded.

Year still after year flows
    down the Seven Rivers;
cloud passes, sunlight glows,
    reed and willow quivers
at morn and eve, but never more
    westward ships have waded
in mortal waters as before,
    and their song has faded.

THE END